Poetry
Introduction
7

GW00724480

Poetry
Introduction
7

faber and faber
LONDON · BOSTON·

First published in 1990
by Faber and Faber Limited
3 Queen Square London WC1N 3AU

Phototypeset by Wilmaset, Birkenhead, Wirral
Printed in Great Britain by
Cox & Wyman Ltd, Reading, Berkshire

A CIP record for this book is available from the British Library

ISBN 0-571-14314-8

CONTENTS

MICHAEL BAYLEY

Trousseau

Thinking you'd gained
strength enough to clear
some of her things
to an upstairs room,

you stand against a bedrail,
visibly shaken
by the lightness of the trunk
holding her wedding dress.

Poltergeist

A glimpse of dad
alone in the living room
after the cleaner had left,

secretly shifting
each ornament and vase
back to where mother had liked them.

The Sandwich Man's Wife

You can see just how starved
she is of a little affection

by the way, when he comes home
sleepwalking, stale as a board,

like the last remains
of some cannibal's tea party,

she removes his crusty socks
and with hands, warm and fat,

tries rubbing back some life
into his raw, tired feet.

By the way she unfastens
the top three buttons of his shirt

and nibbles at his ear.

From Her Sickbed

Tobacco clouds moving
slowly across the globe
in the corner of his study,

watched through a door
left open just wide enough
so he might hear her call.

Floodgates

To begin a story
one seldom needs more
than the necessary amount
of gopher wood

to build an ark,
a very old man,
a zoo and a covenant.

And one can always
pad out a story
with details of flooding:
that it rained cats
and dogs for many days
and nothing survived,
not even the things
that creepeth over the earth,
the element of revenge etc.

But a good ending
is more difficult.
One relies, above all,
on God's good memory,
a dove, an olive leaf
and almost certainly a rainbow.

The Missionary

Wipes his steamed-up specs
with a grubby sleeve,

as if not quite believing
the ten or so cannibals

stood round his boiling pot
can really be murmuring grace

in the passable Antrim brogue
his predecessor, Father Lomax,

a plump yet kindly man,
must have seen fit to teach them.

Last Rites

Late summer, bales
of light fill the room,
cast your shadow on the wall.

I watch you,
looking younger, warmer;
you occasionally sleep.

We alone share
these last hours
of unwilling happiness;

when evening comes
the thin shadow
will enter your body.

Bastille Market

To Sylvia Kantaris

Almost as if gravity
were without its apple,
days took on the lightness

of a sleeping bag
seen hanging as it aired
from a *grenier* window.

Perhaps de Sade,
wearing a silk handkerchief
of untucked lining,

could have carried
the shock of the giant chrysalis
floating from the rooftop,

but for the cauliflower
with its perfect wig,
glancing his foot

and continuing to roll
into the blood and sawdust
of the fish stall.

Hotel Fire in Buenos Aires

To Derek Power

Touched by a match it went up
like the liquid architecture of bees,
the honeycomb lit corridors pumping flame
to the rooftop basketball game
of raised arms madly waving a chopper.

The man on the twentieth storey
must have thought he was dreaming,
jumped as if falling from a tree in sleep,
where final terror, a gentle nudge
or whispering of his name,
might have broken the fall.

El Sol had him frozen in mid-air
on the front cover, along with photos
of the burnt-out shell of the lobby:
black molasses oozing from its timbers,
the crystals of a chandelier
fallen like icicles off the sun.

Nightmare

After she died,
he thought of the horse
they'd always denied her,

even heard it one night,
clip-clopping the landing
in her mother's shoes.

MATTHEW FRANCIS

Morning

Another party. Hot under the lamp she lay.
Winter hit Cambridge yesterday.
The snow is falling on the river.
Ice in the milk. She was so breathlessly

substantial. At such times
I lose the will to work,
gaze out of my window at other windows,
each with its personal Anglepoise

stopped in midspring, frozen.

Waking Late

Three layers of blankets keep the city out.
No curtains hold it back –
already it has entered the room.
When he was a boy,
there was someone to call.
The evening spreads. He is unwell.
Dizziness stops him from appreciating
that weird blue rooftop light he notices,
windows and windows
starting up suddenly in shivering squares,
those white fluorescent rooms.
He turns the pages of a magazine,
December issue. Winter's here.

Soft flash like the discharge of a snowflake.

Still very dark,
    What time is it?
Past three o'clock
    on a cold frosty morning.

What Is a Place?

Somewhere with borders,
e.g., a summer garden,
dogs throbbing, bees
in fierce flowers, burning,
a whole moon left out in the sun.
You waiting for drinks, insects, chill.
The borders, in this case, greens,
strangler figs, grasses, mould smell,
things moving like baboons,
snakes, bushbuck,
in the flora of fringes.
You crossing the streaming path
to the white horizon, the neutral roar,
spray, the continuous ending.
Somewhere that terminates. Look,
here. You have found your place.

Dissolve

The scene is a house in the suburbs,
and the lawn below is set like glass.
The boy on the sill is the same height
as the pane. His left hand holds
his pyjamas crumpled round his waist.
His right holds the white, chipped, wooden
bars with the hard paint. Beyond,
the grass becomes the colour of gnats,
and his father talks in the same tone
to a neighbour across the fence.
Soft flowers of lightning opening
relieve the forms of plants . . .
                  And now,
it's a house in the country,
set amid high translucent cornfields
that run like wax in any wind.
Inside, a log falls in the hearth,
and the father, watching it, shifts
the pewter tankard in his hand.
It is night in the upstairs bedroom,
and the rain starts somewhere beyond
the covers, the colourless language
of rain, uninterrupted by cars.
The boy is a flying island, poised
above, waiting for footsteps
that will be dry, not liquid,
but the shadows run like wax
in the passage . . .
                the dream corridor
breaking up, its inconsequential
conversations cracking into
a hard trickle of mortar, beginning to crunch

on the linoleum –
                    The tearing
of day shows me the shape of a tree
at the window and the gold chain
around your neck –
                    The morning lasts
less than a second, and the tree dies,
leaving its ghost hanging white
on my eyes like memories. Now
is my shape and yours in the lightning
and the tangled voice of the rain
saying nothing that follows. Time
lets the covers slip back, knowing
colour and form, the limits of sleep.
I want to be here when I wake up.

Empire

It is remote here.
Send marmalade.

The Widow Zone*

They have serious problems of integration.
They feel nobody notices them.
Like stranded lines of text,
like ghosts,

standing in alleys under lamp-posts,
unfashionably dressed,
having no option but to disappear,
like a hand seen

opening and closing
on television one Christmas,
they are unconnected.
Rain later.

Between Hilversum and Paris,
the foreign voices come and go,
rising more slowly
on the radio.

*Widow is a printer's term for a line which has become separated from the paragraph to which it belongs.

The Night of the Crab

For Fritz Zorn

After the first injection,
they rolled me on my back
and the sun dried my nerves
and turned my lashes gold . . .
I'm young and rich and educated,
and I'm unhappy, neurotic and alone . . .
Links in the chain.
I couldn't move my head,
watched like a child
as insects multiplied on the page,
carrying a patch of light,
floating, above their bodies,
like meaning . . .
and, of course, I have cancer,
that follows logically enough . . .
A woman's face appeared above me,
moonlike, and I slid
feet first into the sea . . .
This is the night of the Crab
who always withdraws into his loneliness.
He seeks refuge in everything . . .
Pillows, blood, confusion,
still no pain . . .
His planet is the Moon,
he has nothing to do with reality . . .
and then the night-nurse walking
between stately beds.

The great calm.

The Midnight Puffins

I learned much of the world
from the *Children's Encyclopaedia*,
a wheezing Victorian book
that turned the Atlantic

to faded waves,
a cloudy frame
for a puffin it called
the solemn clown of the ocean,

in evening black and white
with smudge-grey bill,
like us, an island dweller,
like us, buoyant with humour.

Pictures were pictures, then,
and life was striped
with unimagined colours.
The puffins of childhood

have settled somewhere,
dardant leur œil rouge,
folded on midnight waves
beside a ruined pier.

Small Hours

1

Gently dip, but not too deep
in the treacle-well of sleep.

When the curtains learn to fly,
gently open half an eye.

Gently, at the knock of rain,
open all the doors again.

Now the clock rings quarter past
something. It is Time at last.

2

One, two, three four five.
Night is only half alive.

Six, seven, eight nine ten.
Time to wake it up again.

Ten, nine, eight seven six.
Back across the River Styx.

Five, four, three two one.
Now look what you've gone and done.

3

Press your ribs against the sheet.
Things are moving in the street.

Who calls old iron door to door?
Someone that you can't ignore.

Clang of iron, cling of rust,
ring the iron angelus.

One, two, three, the shots resound,
but no body will be found.

4

Birds whose voices run with light
shouldn't let it loose at night.

The night-walkers of the town
are sulking in their angled gowns.

All the street signs are in Dutch.
You may see, but do not touch.

All the vowels of all the birds
won't congeal into words.

5

Early risers get to know
the wind that makes their shadows blow,

and the one red trembling star
where the dark is still ajar

but if you wake at quarter past
something, you may guess at last

that there's a day inside the night,
curled inward like an ammonite.

For Creina

The tall damp streets.
The house that climbs
with flaking steps
to another attic,
the tent, the pyramid
where I crouch.
The wreath of bedding
in memory of sleep,
and taxis calling
on the stereo.

Jesus Lane, Parker's Piece, Addenbrookes

And in the street
the wheels of the wind.
Leaking through roof and windows,
the astrological night.
The charted walls,
the tree of life,
the end of the world,
the anatomy of lust.
Bodies imagined,
bodies overheard.
And taxis calling
on the stereo.

Steyne, Elm Grove, Rock Gardens

Nomads who haunt
the spaces between pubs,
the snow-furled darkness,
the darkness stung with stars.

At the end of the street,
the sudden grey horizon,
lights that tingle
with wind, with cold,
and taxis passing.

Where to, love?

Friday Street

As I went down to Friday Street,
the sun was bright in the sky,
the sky was bright in its circle,
the circle of my eye.

As I went down to Friday Street,
the sun was a hammer of gold,
the gardens were open like oysters
when their molten bodies unfold.

And the flowers when I went down there
trembled in purple and blue,
and the sun hammered dust from their petals.
There were people I thought I knew:

a man in the door of a bookshop,
a man in a shining suit,
a mother pushing two babies.
Someone was playing a flute.

The woman who asked me directions
was lost in the heart of July,

and cars with determined expressions
passed expeditiously by.

Two men, two women, two babies,
and one with the sun in his brain,
in a narrow passage of Friday
that opened, then closed again.

It's November on the road northwards.
The door to the bookshop is shut.
All the people have vanished like spiders.
Friday is over. But

elsewhere, a Friday evening
is turning the flowers grey,
and through the 9 p.m. gardens,
a flute is picking its way.

GRAEME HODGSON

A Dead Man

His hair and nails still growing
like they can't accept and if they just
carry on as normal
things will get right again.
   His mother shows remarkable fortitude.
At least they tell her that.
We all know she's one to stop her ears
and hum loudly, which people sometimes
get mixed up with fortitude.
   Really she's in league
with that five o'clock shadow,
that thumbnail pushing on.

Relics

I'm a hoarder myself, I need
the debris of the past, but
my mother's one for clearing the decks.
   Once, I went home and found
my wardrobe almost bare,
except for the old Merchant Navy
reefer and cap.
I said I was surprised
she hadn't got rid of those as well.
She said she couldn't.
Couldn't sell them, that is,
not couldn't bring herself to try.

She'd put an advert in the newsagent's window.
It stayed there a month,
beside the photograph of a lost cat.

The Body

The body washed up
in an unexpected storm
and there was what
they'd all been looking for.

Retching all day,
a steel sea spewed her up,
like it was airing something
pent up over weeks
and it knew how things turn
to poison, kept inside.

Praxiteles' Villa

From inside I could hear
people shifting deadweights
or thumping dust out of linen.
It sounded like the place was
coughing up its ghosts.
I went in.
   Heard workmen cursing
the upright on which he, doggedly,
taught me to play *Clair de Lune*:
I crashed and blundered like a kid
on a first bike, he on the kerb,
shouting balance.
A photograph: it sends him further away,
pompous amateur tenor, tails
like a beetle's folded wings,
mouthing Verdi's *Requiem*.

'Kyrie eleison.
Christe eleison.
Kyrie eleison.'
The wet stench already of must.
Only a week.
The dusty clocks stopped
At some irrelevant minute.
'Lord have mercy on us.
Christ have mercy on us.
Lord have mercy on us.'
His old shopping bag, shabby
as an elephant's ear.

War Stories

She told me how Portsmouth bought it
in the war;
how a bombed house, after rain,
has its own smell.
    She knows about death,
this woman I tend to patronize sometimes.
    We played on similar
landscapes of rubble,
but my streets were demolished,
not bombed.
Recovering footballs, I might find
some treasure overlooked by workmen
but not, as she did,
a hand and a foot in a basin,
forgotten by the wardens.

Living Together

'Great lummox,' she would say.
'Useless bloody fool.'
  In this hateful way
they died together.
  Or else would sit and stare
like lunatics, like pianists,
sculpted in the pose
of their last note.

Removing her rings
to do the washing up,
she places them on the same
window-sill she has placed them on
for sixty-two years,
which is blistered
and tired of rings.

                    *

I recall, lately with humour,
her special hatred of his habit,
when faced with a meal,
of always turning his plate around
before eating, and again when half finished.
'Big dafty,' she would say.
'Always keeps his potatoes East.'

Old Man

He talks of way back.
When footballs
had laces
and lungs.

He is back
in the old home,
dreaming of a boy
who plays alone
in the shallow stream,
where a cold
and pure water
chatters trivia
all day.

Nana

The first thing she did every morning
was drink a glass of hot, boiled water.
She said it flushed you through.
Sleeves rolled up, in her own house, she drank it.

*

As it dawned, it was the look
of surprise, tightening
across her cool, kissed temples
that I remember most.
Mam telling her about
the all-round convenience
and the new friends she would make.

And there were other things:
only last week she forgot the kettle.
She will never forget the kettle now,
the way it frets on the blue jet.
Turn your back too long, she knows,
and it will be rattling with
dry conspiracies.

I heard that the house was rented now
by a group of polytechnic students.
Recently I contrived to pass that way.
Through the window I noticed the familiar
wallpaper that everyone mucked in to hang,
partly covered now with posters.
Bowie in the weird days.
A 'Militant' sticker in the corner
of the mirror which every
morning misted over, sharing
a clear toast.

Aunties

I remember my aunties
like old leather things.
   Not unkindly.
I once thought they were born
wearing floral printed pinnies,
pressed and spotless,
protecting shabby dresses.
Like dust jackets folded
round heavy old tomes.
   It was uncles I lacked.

Or forget.
What remains is the smell of bleach
in the kitchens of round widows,
who died.

Waiting Room

People in doctors' waiting rooms
very often don't look ill at all.
This little boy does though.
I notice him concentrating too hard
on the tank of tropical fish,
trying to ignore some sickness
which is deep in him.
You can see that he might die.

The fish don't seem too bothered though.
Glazed in, they've seen it all before
and stared back just the same.
He watches them, less intently,
as they motor up and down the tank,
absurdly out of scale with the sunken galleon
(which is absurdly out of scale
with the 'No Fishing' sign).
Turning away, his shoulders say
that he knows about depending
on others for cleaning and a machine
which makes bubbles.

The Dead

I

He sits there.
Or lies there.
Forgetting.
Once he was red and grumpy,
a real grandad.
Now we watch him
in case he falls,
or burns the place down
with that bloody pipe.

II

I can see us there,
admiring the flowers:
things he never cared for.
Quick winds, scratching umber leaves
round the measured plots;
tugging at umbrellas and anoraks
with the sound of sail.
  I can see him in that daft silk shift
which formed part of the lining of the box.
He would have cringed to see himself dead in it.
I wanted his waxy lips to whisper:
'Well, young man.
Come and kiss my draughty brows,
come and kiss my paler face.'
He would have said nothing of the sort.

Institution

Out in twos they emerge
from a hidden door.
They all wear the same black shoes.
Are all clothed in boiled linen.
Five circuits of the courtyard and back inside.
An old hand once told me that a shift of mood
was discernible after the noon exercise period.
The change though was a subtle one,
like that to be seen between people
entering and leaving a restaurant.

By five o'clock
all two thousand and seventy-three faces
are lined each side of four huge trestle tables,
stained with many meals.
All the white faces hung like silent canvases,
the long galleries of an entire movement.
Food moves on aluminium . . .
is lifted slowly among them.

DAVID MORLEY

Thirteen Ways of Avoiding the Blackbird

I

Among twenty snowy tower-blocks
the only seeing thing –
the black nib of a pen.

II

A man and a woman
are one.
A man and a woman and a blackbird
is an arrestable offence.

III

I was of one mind
like a crowded room
in which there is one television.

IV

I know noble accents –
their inert, escapist rhythm;

but I know, too,

I was undermined
by what I knew.

V

I do not know which to prefer –
the fineness of her inflections,
or the finesse of her innuendoes –

the PM rejoicing
or just after.

VI

Data force-feeds the machine
with incomprehensible lines.
The shadow of the ribbon
crossed itself, to and fro.

Truth
tears through the page

– unmistakable claws.

VII

The river is moving –
Sellafield must be changing shift.

VIII

When the swing-wing flashed out of sight

it tore the edge
of many silences.

IX

O thin men of Mammon,
why do you imagine golden birds?

Do you not see the mamba
curling through the hearts
of children about you?

X

The chopper-blades whirled in the acid winds –
last part of the pantomime.

XI

At the sight of locusts
flying in green light,

even in the bunker
will they cry out sharply.

XII

She rode over everything –
everything –
in a white coach.

But once a fear pierced her,
in that she mistook
the shadows of her country

for wings of blackbirds.

XIII

It was evening all afternoon.

It was snowing
black snow.

The blackbird

burning

in cedar-limbs.

Climbing Zero Gully

For P.C., killed while climbing Ben Nevis, 1982

There is no cut rock
but terrified stones
keeping the peace,
unchallenging.

They challenge:
perusing second-pitch belay,
scribing snake-backs in the snow,
hard as glacier,

the piton correcting itself
almost self-consciously.
Hand and over-hand, they jerk
upwards and on,

absolutely competent, nursed
by Japanese equipment.

On comes a night,
bleating, unchallenging.

Rock: screw-faced and water-brained.
They: complete in mountain-power
stand, chin in hand,
suddenly vigilant.

Air Street

Deer-tracks – I followed them: made
a forest slide through a deer's eye; felt

for myself the trodden dints of hoof,
shorthand codes cut on the frost . . .

Pitch of night: insurgent shrews
scatter in dissidence between owls.

My torch-beam welds them to the ground:
I could gather them like moss.

The air as well, corrupt with movement,
walks with me like gravity

and, step-by-step, it flenses sound
to whispers of a deer-cut.

Where the tracks street together –
passes of a scalpel –

with torch-light off, eyes wide for catlight,
I smelled their musks like creosote

and saw the deer – a herd of ten –
scent me there, *and go*.

Morning took me southwards; levelled on fat
curving rails, restive station platforms,

ticks of rain. As if trespassing
I cut the close-wire of people.

Gun-dogs grabbed me at traffic-lights.
Gamekeepers in Downing Street

met my stare.
It was night delivered me this:

a street lit by nothing –
near where I could sleep –

with a name like nothing: *AIR*.
And I walked it without torch-light

sensitive for the wear of previous creatures.

Second Sight

Birds to a bird-table:
our neighbours' greedy sympathy

on seeing the curtains shut all summer,
strangers call by . . .

Inside, my mother's book-lust
spread like weed; paraquat titles:

The World, The Flesh, The Devil,
back copies of *Which?*.

At twelve, I paired *Walpurgis*
with 'the latest in slow cookers',

furthered the *First Cause,*
that consumer's aphorism.

No surprise to find her
watchdog of the Tarot,

sifting pictures
tenderly like photographs.

Her dregs of Typhoo
a cup of darkness, the Tarot

opened futures
where she held all the cards . . .

Then, registered, I fingered
our bad address

in *Romany Index* '77,
listing: 'coven'.

Suddenly we were graduates;
thunder nailed-up messages;

November's flood
brought a flotsam of fresh business.

Curled in similar grace,
I pretended an inheritance:

served tea like sacrament,
picked warts off the seed-cake.

That first seance was nerveless
cathartic giggles;

we re-tuned our hands like surgeons,
pulled up the dead like floorboards.

Who was it derailed us? –
that First of May when,

closeted with props,
herbs *de rigueur*,

you called up your lover
from a deaf basement,

the only sound,
the sound of his resistance?

Errand

I came to a place where buildings were going up;
biscuits of slate sat wrapped in twine.

Earth moved like sugar, boiling
against the metal of a dumper.
A machine dropped, dropped its yellow snout,
nuzzling at joists
it hammered-in.
When I got to my father I would learn
the heat of that impact, how you might
light paper from it two hours on . . .
The air meanwhile would shiver with fire,
a fineless dust, the shouts of impact.

He was with the welders –
short-term hire – cutting thin plate
to microns. Not visored, he
stood out from that coven
of kneeled and sparking men
like something they were making
or melting to start over.
We went out to sandpiles, pounded stone,
his eyes spindling, his mouth
asking and asking why I was there.

On Fire

When, on withering into life, smoke
chances on opacity, there

seems a kind of rock
cut from the sharpest energies

in fire: a compliancy, a pliant stone
of smoke, a broken form

turned blunt-end to the ground . . .
Stoking up, you flesh that sparse

contracted source. The flame-points swell
with wings and cobbled smoke.

Masking a fist, you weave in half-burnt wood –
tuff of lichens to fissure in fire –

and stand away, watching how
the falling-up of heat

quarries air of flakes and finity.

A sculptor works less openly,
releasing stone in secret,

scraping through caves to find a captive,
hands like drills. The binds of stone

shrivel to his touch: a plying flame
as fumbles out of smoke. He makes

his fist a phoenix; hands he turns
are wings that clench a fire,

a beak that bites
is chisel in this stone . . .

The warm wings lift
a trembling limb from rock:

a dust, like smoke, veers into air.

Jackdaw Blues

I select my best shotgun – a Berren ·22.
I'm a Monaghan farmer. I've got work to do.

Jackdaws are prickling the edge of my mind.
I'm tired of vermin and I'm tired of time.

The crops rise up like sentries there.
You can't whistle money out of thin air.

These birdies are shillings to throw away.
I can take their begging, but I take my pay.

Over the border, the prices are low.
Those beaks in my wallet have to go.

I'd a son shot by terrorists over the way.
Like, he was begging. They blew him away.

Sometimes I wonder if they feel the shot
before the gun-crack scatters the lot.

I'm begging too – a gun is my prayer.
I can make dust like God. Yes, out of thin air.

Them jackdaws squat black: dead fruit on my trees.
I remember the priest: his gaggle of fees.

I remember the missus . . . she moved as she died
towards the priest's hand. He squatted and sighed.

One death such as this won't add to the others,
he murmured. He'd forgotten my brother's.

The gun on my arm won't steady if I cry.
The gun in my heart's self-loaded till I die.

Sentry Hill: A Story

The brother died young, at home;
the child in the yellow photograph,

restored and sneering in your room.
Too often you would talk about his music

– the ignored fugues mouldering,
locked in a suitcase beneath his bed –

and decided that some other misunderstood
genius was rewriting them this very moment

if any of this were actually true.

I love him without knowing him.
No one remembered him but you.

I don't ask any questions; now
there is no point, now I am alone to know

of his existence: washed-up
on the dreg of a small Ulster farm.

And yet you will say, as Montale
once whispered, *how easy it is*

to love a shadow, myself always
trying to be shadow

if any of this were true.

Kiss

In the mechanism of a child's throat:
a template of staves, octaves, baby-talk
bubbles, poetries of attention-seeking . . .
The hurting side is gone, but in my mind
Heather is still there, a baby.
The sawn edge of a shotgun, seething
through a caravan's ersatz coat –
rabid, percussive . . . *When you find*
your child like that, quiet, as though she
had dreamed through it all, you want to walk

up to the fuckers who did it, and burn them slowly.
Sunlight topples the last galleries of Divis;
a bus grinds fuel on the grass of Falls.
(He will burn them slowly, atom by atom.)
I knelt to kiss her, then I saw the flex
trailing from her wrist to her legs . . .
A mirror of sheet-iron crashes
from the roof of Unity Flats. (He
wanted to kiss her, atom by atom;
atom by atom, to dream through it all . . .)

Long Division

11 p.m., and Kellogg's Bran Flakes still occupy
their place of honour on the only
table. Dusk: the clapboard partitions
tack each room to a hierarchy of radio stations.

We could do worse . . . The Beijing physicist
lectures me on marriage, his
Habitat wok drying on the light-flex. At night
he murders bedsprings with X'an, his sub-atomic expert.

After dinner, falling to print, *New Scientist*
warns me there is only this
last particle to uncover, (but goes on)
how we are just that one

unthought-of matter multiplied:
think of a number, double it.
Creation's trick's
that way of filing down to this

from grasses, water – Dada art –
lost foundations; do not start
one city or one single stone
before the central sum is known.

I walked with you in Belfast's core –
are we like them? Crack pushers toured
in soft-lit hatchbacks, tail-lights down;
they sometimes slowed, but caught your frown,

shifting up gear.
A gang of punks
exploded from falling glass,
scattering fear . . .

I want to run with them.

PAUL MUNDEN

A New Arrival

When I imagined the Big Time it was not
in the basement of Broadcasting House
stepping up between Peter Porter
and Anthony Thwaite to the white urinal.

*

Paul Munden, Paul Muldoon. Hugh, you
introduced us over a glass of wine,
your mulled voice muddling the occasion.
I was a wisp, while the maestro was –
dare I say it – well-heeled, plump
as a prize mushroom. He leaned forward
to catch my name again, stumbling
on another of his magical half-rhymes.

*

The promotion was half-baked.
It was a double bill
and Selima's photo read Adams
not Hill.

I was putting her up
for the night. It was late, and when
we got back you'd gone to bed.
You'd also gone to town

on our country kitchen
with french bread, cheese,
and a giant hand-made plate of fruit
like a stiff napkin, topped with strawberries.

Strange for the two of you
to meet first over breakfast.
In just a few more weeks we'd have
a regular, little-known guest.

Skiffle

The bass is a long piece of elastic
stretched on a broomstick.
An empty barrel of home-brew
doubles as a drum

and this is just the formal set.
You're free to join in
with an improvised maraca –
that handy jar of rice.

My baby daughter beats
not-quite-time with a wooden spoon
on a saucepan: I click a pen
against my teeth.

Can you picture all this?
I lack the studio's big budget
to put it on celluloid
before your very eyes –

my word will have to do.
It's not much, I admit. Sometimes
the sound carries no further
than this room.

The Little Nipper

Happy Chris Mouse. Marketing's gift
for turning the seasonal language
into slush was luckily lost on you.
Your fingers scrabbled at the eyes,
the cherry nose, fluffing the rosy cheeks.
We moved the dining-table out

and brought in an old settee from the barn
to make a comfortable playroom.
What worried us was worm
but the next day's evidence –
tissue paper pinked into a ragged doily –
suggested our pests were furry friends.

The local hardware store supplied me
with 'The Little Nipper'. I cut a square
of cheese and lodged it on the spike,
the steel spring snapping forward
several times before it was triggered.
I dreamed that sound all night.

And in the morning, there he was,
jaw squashed by the steel,
eyes still locked in a black stare.
I put you safely behind bars
with your monster-sized cuddly toy.
'Play with that while I deal with this.'

I lifted the trap complete with victim
dangling by the nose but the tail
brushed the back of my hand

and a shiver scooted up my arm and around
my shoulders. You liked the glow
in the coals as I tossed it on the range.

That's What This Is

You lunge, lock on to the teat of your bottle
like a little prop forward into the scrum,

and you look the part in your stripes,
with mauled ears, chubby cheeks; thin on hair . . .

You found your feet – there they were
all the time! How long before I'm telling you

to pull up your socks? Already the struggle is on
for independence. Breakfast is the battleground.

I offer a finger of toast but you want the piece
on my plate. I let you taste it in order to believe

it's one and the same thing. You catch sight
of yourself in the mirror: an identical baby

smiles out. It's all so hard to grasp. Toys
do help, with chunky controls, mechanics

that a microchip could handle in its sleep.
Push that lever and Humpty Dumpty's head slices

off into your lap. Pull this, and you bring
my own forgotten childhood back to life.

Shared memory is as much of a bond as the bond
of the flesh. My father's gone

but his friend of some seventy years tells me
how they once shared a desk. It could be yesterday.

Mnemonics

1

Chapel. Given free bibles by some God Squad freaks.
No haircut but History prep foul. Life-saving a shag.
Stutchbury will almost definitely swap the stamps.

*

Orchestra not bad but we know the pieces too well.
Started to hatch brine shrimps which I don't think
will work. Sixth in triple jump though nearly second.

*

Painted an old ammunition box to keep my stamps in.
Captain Noah. If only I could sing in a deep voice
like the others. Skived. No bath as they were full.

*

English. Essay on aftermath of atomic explosion.
Wrote eight pages! I think I might make it the end
of a book I might write. Electrified my violin.

*

Charted the evolution of life, then table tennis.
It seems Finding has half cut his arm off, so
our entry in the Music Comp is slightly up creek.

*

Looked for stamp hinges but found other things
instead. Captain Noah. I don't want to do a woman.
Thai might be going back to Vietnam next term.

*

The brine shrimps have hatched! Hot dogs and cider
after the concert. Broke milk bottles for a laugh.
History revision. Mr Penny is a swine. Wrote diary.

2

Two is for second-hand, I'm afraid. What we need
here are reproductions of the photos in question
but the publishers couldn't run to it, or wouldn't.

In any case, I'm not convinced. Past girlfriends
stay a pretty eighteen. When I took no holiday snaps,
friends refused to believe I'd had a good time.

Now their correspondence has lapsed to enlargements
of the latest small. Stricter than any governess
the viewfinder shapes them up; the be-all, the end-

Paradise Lost

'One step beyond *Star Wars*
and *Close Encounters of the Third Kind*,
based on the book by John Milton
from an original idea by God,
Chaos Films proudly present . . .'

It never reached production. Finance
fell through, the Writers' Guild
wrangled over credits
and casting was always a problem.

Pandemonium really set in
when the director, a stickler for detail
and playing devil's advocate,
suggested Latin dialogue.
The poet would have approved, he said.
Why else did the guy write in English
if not to alienate
the international audience of his day?

One Picture is Worth a Thousand Words

Books have never been the same
since dinosaurs stopped popping up
from behind cardboard trees
and the lines of text, once found only
in the very top or bottom margin,
began to scamper all over the page.

*

Two moon-faces chortle
through the froth of their beer,
glued to a juicy page three.
(.)(.) News
is squeezed into the wings.

*

Don't underestimate a literate script.
One blockbuster's wordage grosses as much
as all those art-house flops
I could cite as *auteur*.
Personally, I don't even have a TV.
That? Oh, the VDU – receives only
my signals, nothing from the outside world.

Honeymoon

We were the last of our species visible
along the vast length of the beach. The sun
still shone out of season, if too weakly
for most. The tinny Suzuki scuffed
through the sand – we wore no helmets, sure
of a soft fall.
                        You'd reached the end
of the only book you had. We tried sharing
my page but I was far too slow so we tore
The French Lieutenant's Woman in half.
You began while I finished, and for once,
reading didn't seem the usual rift.
The sun thinned. We returned to the hotel
and pushed the narrow twin beds back together.

Testudo

1 (After Evelyn Waugh)

Embedded diamonds spell the girl's name.
A living casket – it skids
on the polish and is put back to GO.

'What will you do when it is dead?'
asked Mr Samgrass. 'Can you have
another tortoise fitted to the shell?'

Don't laugh: these things happen.
But I wonder if my pain, grafted
to another's, will shrivel or swell?

2 (After T. H. White)

The story has it, that all ships
go more slowly when carrying
the right foot of a tortoise on board.

So when the wind dropped
and the lumbering stowaway was found
below deck, your course was clear.

But you were worried, not knowing
your right from your left,
so you chopped off the other two too.

3 (After Sydney Smith)

'Why, boy, are you stroking the tortoise?
To please it? Child! You might as well stroke
the dome of St Paul's to please the Dean!'

My vague, naïve beliefs hold firm.
The body houses the spirit, and the church
is the house of God. My sluggish schooling

shuns your elegant wit, and a word –
Latin of all things – is reassembling
in my brain. *Religio*: I connect.

The Practice Room

His voice was a stony bass, rinsed
with meths. One side of his cassock
sagged with the tell-tale bottle's weight
and when he leaned across to turn
the page, I was jabbed by the smell.

His hands were yellow ivory, his fingers
exacting hammers. In the dingy practice room
he taught me Hindemith but my progress
was slow, still is. I explained
how I had to divide my time with the violin

at which he took my hands
and felt the flexible knuckles revolve
in their oil. I try it myself now
and it just won't work.

*

The room became her Victorian parlour.
She came and went like a ghost,
her grey hair a frizzed silhouette
against the window, beyond which
other boys played cricket in the yard.

She believed in letting the bow ride free.
Before, you had to hold – and later imagine –
a book under the arm. All this
she said in a whispering vibrato
that seemed to brush my skin.

It's been a long time. My violin slides out
from a silk scarf. We uncork the wine.
The piano gives an A for me to crank
the stiff pegs up to the mark.

ROBERT SAXTON

Reflections

A Tabloid for the Wee Small Hours

Live Letters

Tell me (my schooling's full of holes)
What firemen use to grease their poles.

I' truth, sir, no grease keeps 'em slick:
The firemen's trousers do the trick.

Teacher praised who plimsolled rumps.
Quick, lads! All hands man the pumps!

Let's give the metalwork a shine!
The flames lick round the plimsoll line.

Star Wrinkles

Keep vigil with insomniac rust.
Open the telly: meet the dust.

Break bread with the brave bright mouse
Whose wee black pellets dot the house.

Shall the sigh wear out its sheath,
The teacher or the fire chief?

The moon looks blankly on their throes,
Turns on love its cold white hose.

Hard heart, soft bargain: play it rough.
The valves accumulate their fluff.

Baby, You're so Friable

Boffins agreed on cranial sumps.
It seems brain cells sheer off in lumps,

Not slow depletion byte by byte –
Great colonies lost overnight

Like tons of chalky cliff that slide
Quietly into the nibbling tide.

The Promise Clinic

First Day

They flutter on the eye,
A mild surprise,
Like prices on books
Lent long ago
You thought you'd never see again.

But more than these
The thickening of ghosts
You'd starved of light.
Who would have guessed
They'd interview so well?

Second Day

First, all the whisky's under lock and key.
You can smell tomorrow's weather,
Hear your babbling bloodstream, see
A corkscrew hair trapped in the cleaner's charm bracelet.

She swabs and jingles her way across your floor,
Out of your room and down the corridor.
You're alone. Now try this for size:
Your first, worst marriage, whole before your eyes.

Lawn Aerator Sandals

Today in the Gardeners' Hyperdome
I sauntered along the avenues admiring,
Right and left, ingenious flimsy things for gardening.
I'm sure you would have seen the charm
Of the pair of lawn aerator sandals with screw-in tines,
The kind of present you might have bought – two pairs – for
                                        our new home,
Whose lawn we could have aerated walking up and down,
                                        arm in arm,
Enjoying the cherry blossom. They were designed to strap
Over ordinary shoes, my size elevens and your incredible size
                                        fours,
Which on train journeys you would beg me to pull up on my
                                        lap,
Undo and remove to massage your feet.

And bouncing on their bamboo poles,
Responsive to the breeze from automatic doors,
Morning's Minions, the rubberized kestrel bird scarers
We could have posted round the cherry trees in flocks
To scare real birds away. And should our turf
Have proved a habitat for inconsiderate moles,
Why not a battery-powered device whose drun-drun-drun of
                                        shocks

Below ground would have sent them scuttling to the next
postcode
With a ringing in their ears? Too cruel, I hear you say.
You would happily have watched our too well-aerated lawn
Like a building site accumulate soil by the cartload.
It's obvious to me that moles, like birds, are vandals.
But if you had thought that moles were underfoot,
I doubt if we ever would have worn
Our lawn aerator sandals.

Devil's Prothalamion

Brace the will to take the strain.
Weigh the in-laws with the bride.
Lies enlarge inside the brain.

Damn the Abel with the Cain,
Fell the Jekyll with the Hyde.
Brace the will to take the strain.

Scotch the hymeneal stain
That claws its way from side to side.
Lies enlarge inside the brain.

Check the harvest grain by grain,
Cheat the bloating of the tide.
Brace the will to take the strain.

Both sides of the counterpane
The clans are grouping where you lied.
Lies enlarge inside the brain.

Plan to catch the stopping train.
Let self-protection be your guide.
Lies enlarge inside the brain.
Brace the will to take the strain.

A Motel Room Near St Austell

. . . when you do dance, I wish you
A wave o' the sea, that you might ever do,
Nothing but that, move still, still so,
And own no other function.
                    The Winter's Tale

Venetian blinds are battened,
Though it's only just turned noon.
The bedside globe is smooth and white –
A prelapsarian moon.

The duvet's docile on the floor,
The hollow in the sheet's still warm.
A tigress, or a giant hare,
Has just this minute left its form.

Unseen, the mountains hoard their myths,
Benign, spectral, recondite.
Their useless gifts are bobbing near,
Borne in on tides of light.

Her shape, like Parian when still,
Is flowing now across the room
Towards her weightless underwear.
She flickers in the milky gloom,

And to such flickering one is drawn,
Like hand to fur, or cup to lip.
Where I had meant to smooth, I scare,
And drown where she had thought to sip.

The Makeshifter Calls

He was an hour late
   and that was an hour of worry.
Nothing was going right
   and no one was even saying sorry.

Everything was makeshift, unreliable,
   as I'd explained to my GP,
   whose Freudian face and lovely surgery
   (Victorian globe, leather books, serpentine couch)
   had made me think, naïvely, he might be of some use to me.

So I'd looked in the *Yellow Pages*
   and chosen the largest, most pictorial ad,
   a firm with three telephone numbers and the prefix Euro-.
We never close, all credit cards taken, it said.

He turned up at the same time
   as my notorious on-the-run lover.
His leather case was scarred like a favourite toy
   and smeared with butter from his previous call
   where he'd amiably plonked it on the tea table,
   over the muffins, before pulling out
   all his little springs you attach yourself to the future by.

A Malachite Egg

Now I know what the egg means: it's a
living thing before it has time to get messy.

Two ponies stand
Perfectly still,
Head to tail,
Tail to head,
Each tail
In its turn
Swishing flies away.

We are in a lane
Two fields
From the cliff edge,
Smiling goodbye,
Face to face,
Our bicycles
Enforcing distance.

I remember this,
Sitting alone
In my kitchen,
Weighing in my palm
The cold object,
Weighing in my mind
Its wavy stripes

In two shades
Of green,
Its singleness,
Its perfect hold

On time,
And this evening
When I walk

Along the beach,
Crunch by crunch
I shall
Turn over,
Like the waves
The pebbles,
This first promise.

River Red with Berries

In Wildman's Wood a river flows,
A river red with berries.

Where is she gone, where is she gone?
And why is she away so long?

She's picnicking in Wildman's Wood
On leaves of hornbeam, oak and beech,
Which all taste best when they are brown.
(Remember she was old and thin
And couldn't keep her supper down?)
She's picnicking the branches clean.

When will she come back again?
I miss her, so I need to know.

When will she come back again?
When the river runs milky with melted snow.

High Becquerel Farm

This is my den,
The oiling pen
Where sheep are oiled
Against the wind –

Or so I said
To little Ted,
The townie
Staying on our farm.

It was quiet, to say
It was a bank holiday.
Ted knew why: this year
Everyone had gone to Chernobyl.

We sat there in the cold,
The ruined fold
Hugged round us
Like a blanket.

Damned if I'd show
Him my patch of snow
The winter had left behind,
Dirtier than ever,

Or my favourite tarn
The Innominate Tarn
All churned up
Like the view from a galleon.

Caveat Emptor

Some books, however thin,
Refuse to fit back in their slot.
That's when a friend will zero in
Across the bookshop floor
And put you on the spot.
Oh yes, what's this? A present? Who's it for?

Your secret self, that's who;
And so you feel just as you might
If the shower were to run dry, leaving shampoo
On your hair, helmet of foam,
And you with just a squash racket to fight
A dragon on the bus ride home.

JONATHAN TREITEL

I Want the State to Construct Me

I want the State to construct me
in the dead of winter
in the form of a statue
striking a revolutionary posture
carved out of ice.

In the spring, I will drip,
drip, drip . . . And the young
will come and sit
on my pedestal (dampish,
a bit, perhaps, and fringed
with moss) and complain.

The Foundry

1

Ghetto means 'foundry' –
a peripheral island where a pot of mulled steel
was drawn into swords, book-chains, flowerpot-hooks,
the V-shaped reinforcement of a gondola's prow.
The black-red glow having flickered
out finally, this slaggy patch
was granted to the first Jews in Venice.
In the beginning, the word was *gietto*,
but it has come down to us in a mangled version:
these immigrants from the Franco-German
Holy Roman Empire couldn't manage the alien
initial consonant, they couldn't force
their tongue and jaw to emit that grating *jjj*:
harsh grind of the huge gate's hinges.

2

If you follow the arrow on the signpost, descending
from the hurly-burly of the railway station complex
through the *sottopassaggio*
(the abrupt black tunnel)
's narrowing walls,
and you turn
at the end, below where the darkened arch
bumps into sunshine, and glance sideways, you will see
the original dent where the old gates hung.
You will have the urge
(each passer-by before you
has rubbed a finger round the rim)
to reach out and touch.
Now it is quite shiny.

3

A silver amulet from the sixteenth century –
glittery in places, tarnished in places,
crimped here and there for decorative effect
or as a result of much rough squeezing
at instants of outrageous hope or terror –
swung from a chain round somebody's neck.
It rose between her breasts
when she arose;
laid down when she lay down.
Now it rests on a velvet cushion,
absorbs stares.
A Name of God engraved thereon
is misspelled by carelessness or deliberately
to avert the Evil Eye.

4

Portabessamim they called it in a word
half Italian and half Hebrew.
It is a speculation in pierced silver:
a toy pillbox fortification, or an abstract
elongated octahedral think-piece, or a detached
miniaturized turret from Solomon's temple
flying a brave stiff flag. It exists
to be sniffed. At the close of Sabbath,
each member of the family leaned into
its scent and was reconciled
to the profane working week. You can smell
nothing now. But once it was crammed with
cloves, allspice, cinammon – an aroma imported
from Palestine or thereabouts.

5

Somebody's grandfather remembers a few words
of the old Ghetto argot – a tohu-bohu
of Hebrew, Ladino and Venetian Italian –
that *his* grandfather mumbled to him;
and he keeps coming out with it
at inconvenient moments, puzzling the visitors.
His embarrassed grandchildren shush him silently
by grace of a complex of Italian hand gestures.
He takes this for applause of a kind.
Sometimes, like a bright baby, he can
actually string together a whole phrase,
a proverb that was chanted over his crib:
Ki de goyim sfida, hazirii a:
'If you trust the goyim, they'll stuff you with pig.'

6

They would paddle their shallow barges
through winding canals, pushing off from banks
with a spare hand, easing away, and bowing low as they
passed
beneath the slick green underside of a bridge.
They would call out for
any old clothes. Any old clothes
(holed stockings or grubby jerkins),
assessed, selected, bought, collected, washed, sorted,
patched, stored,
were put on offer during the return voyage.
Whosoever has died or is growing out of youth
has some to dispose of.
Whosoever is born or is growing into adulthood
has need of some.
Six days a week, the barges went round.

7

In the reign of Napoleon, the curfew was abolished.
The gates of the Ghetto were torn from their hinges
by iron-hungry scrap-metal dealers,
carted elsewhere, smelted, forged into cannon.
At last the Jews were free to row through the canals leading
into
the lagoon, after sunset; look back
at their own homes, the little oil lamps flickering.
Soon after, came the railway along the causeway from the
mainland;
engines breathed sparks near the Ghetto walls.
More steel: more fire.

Foundries are everywhere, and the Jews
do not live within the old constraints.
Roads lead in and out. You can no longer tell
where the Ghetto ends and where the world begins.

Dog in Jerusalem

The loudest racket in the Old City
after dusk, louder

than the *muezzin* at his megaphone
or Hassidim at singsong,

is the yowl of an Alsatian
unkennelled but tethered

on top of the roof
of a rusty tumbledown shack

on top of the roof
of an Arab market.

Nowhere else to put it,
I suppose.

Up there,
it can hardly be guarding anything.

But the dog doesn't know.
He thinks he is protecting

the whole black night set with stars.

A Marble in Jerusalem

Here's a glass marble rolling
along a dry gutter in the centre
of the Jewish quarter of the Old City.

One clear drop,
no larger or smaller than an eye;
a blue whirl is trapped.

A child had been playing with it
in the Christian ghetto. It had dropped
through a skylight into

the Muslim market;
been kicked by random feet
up to the cobbled courtyard

of the Armenian cathedral;
bounced down stone steps,
an archway, a rat hole,

and along a dry gutter
into the very centre
of the Jewish quarter.

Sabbath.
The world is quiet and small.
Crazy blue sky, though.

Mobilization

No, no human was to blame, blame,
if you must, the Aachen Hauptbahnhof . . .
There was a day in August 1914, when
the helter-skelter onrush into war almost
paused, the Kaiser almost
ordered his army to hold back
at the Belgian frontier
but did not.

You see, the troop-trains kept rolling
into the frontier station, and there weren't
enough sidings to huddle them in;
once the forces were mobilized,
where else was there for them to go
except onwards, across the border?

Reach

The arabesque of slit trenches, the graceful
zigzag of sandbags crisscrossing the line of fire,
'firebay' and 'parados' in mazy intricacy,
the niches, the recesses,
the fine art of concealment . . .

darkness; a soldier with outstretched arms sleepwalking,
                                        wanting
just his beloved, trying, trying
to touch and be touched . . .

An American colonel wrote to his wife:
'Darling, take a good look at the ground,
when I get home, you won't be seeing it for a long time.'

He died. And she
looked at the ground
and didn't see it for a long time.

Hide and Seek

Where does the stress go in *camouflage*?
young British officers mumbled
at the beginning of the Great War.
They soon got the hang of it.
This foreign polysyllable infiltrated into English.

Drury Lane backdrop painters were taken on
to do up lorries with abstract landscapes
in the swirly style of the later, madder Van Gogh
or chopped-up Cézanne strokes.
The theatre of war was fitted out
with false artillery of silver birch trunks.

And snipers curled
behind a scrim of green gauze stuck with leaves
like in the pantomime of *Babes in the Wood*.

Bricklaying for You

The tingle must go on the tingle-plate
so the wind won't blow the line off true
and upset the perfection of the course.
You can sight it by eye. The cement
comes ready-mixed and should not be
dried out. Check this. Next, in a fluent
scoop, take a level trowelful
from the hand-hawk to the stretcher-frog,
slap it and scrape it. End the row
with a queen-closer or a double-bullnose.
I expect you will have completed
the shebang by knocking-off time. Then let us go
home together for an Ovaltine and a Kit-Kat.

In our next lesson, we will build
an arch out of bricks. *Impossible*,
you think. But it is just a matter of placing
the voussoirs between the intrados and the extrados.

An Interpretation of Dreams

'For the eternal dignity of the human Soul, and against the
glorification of Instinct, we hereby burn the books of Freud.'
    Declaration at an incineration ceremony, Vienna, 1939

Begin with a Moravian birthplace: a serious boy stroking
what would be his beard if he had one, while cutting
human figures from sheet metal in the neighbourhood
locksmith's shop. And end in a vacant consulting room
in suburban London; amid the statuettes of Anubis
and the framed testimonials: a yapping chow.

Insert *The Interpretation of Dreams*, and a book on jokes,
and a dozen gross of cigars, and the first jaw twinges of 1917
(which he supposed psychosomatic) and thirty-three
                                                    operations
to cut out carcinomic lumps not unrelated to cigar smoke,
which leads on to eels: his 1877 seminal work on their
'paired grooved lobulated organ in the abdominal cavity'.

Permanent pain from the palatal prosthesis –
nicknamed 'The Monster'. Add a World War or two,
rebellious disciples, addiction to cocaine, punctured
knowallishness, bad breath, a dead musical mother, and you
                                                        have
an inflammable mixture: just toss in a naked flame and *woof!*
goes the chow, doing its business on the couch.

'Every analyst must himself be analysed,' – so who
was the first, then – or an infinite regression? He was
an eminence from a past epoch, which tipped over for good
or bad on the 1st January 1900, when he wrote:
'The one thing we know for sure about the coming century,
is that it contains the date of our death.'

Chamber of Horrors

Blue eyes ran out
during World War Two.
The sole manufacturer
was a Bohemian glassworks;
after the Sudetenland fell,
it was only a matter of time.

Madame Tussaud's
was reduced to mimicking
swarthier notables.
But the public objected
to incessant brown and grey.
At last, the artists

cannibalized the unwanted
waxen skulls
of lesser aristocrats
guillotined during the Terror.
They prised out the eyeballs
with a sharpened teaspoon.

and inserted matched pairs
into Churchill (complete
with authentic cigar)
and Princess Elizabeth
on her azure-eyed
Shetland pony.

Extract from
Mrs Potter Remembers Some Nice Moral Tales

1 About My Very Nice Skin

Oh I had the smooth skin when I was a little
snip of a girl in my pinny and giggle;
passing gentlemen used to pass and admire it
for miles around, in particular Dr Morecombe;
gather up handfuls of my face, till I couldn't bear it
any longer, he would; he was partial to some

nice bit of cheek. He smelled of drink.
I told him No. He asked Why. I said Because.
So I grew up, and he stopped it. I know you think
it was, but it wasn't. Or maybe it was.

Moral

You've got to take (what he always said) the smuff with the
                                                         rooth.
Oh and it got him in the end, Dr Morecombe, the booze.

JONATHAN WONHAM

Alzhbeta

(Adapted from Milan Kundera's 'Symposium')

Nurse Alzhbeta dances for Doctor Havel,
for Doctor Havel is like death.
He takes everything.

Alzhbeta's fingers
that have rummaged festering wounds
dowse the damp restrictions
of her pale blue uniform.
With a gaze that is blank as the sun
she moves her slow thighs,
posing in the full glory
of her fictional nakedness.

The five staff-room characters
constitute an audience
worse than any Viennese strip joint,
yet Alzhbeta removes
her fictional lingerie, throwing
each slice of whalebone and lace
to the doctors, her colleagues.
'Flaishman,' she cries, 'you milksop, you dropped it!'

Nurse Alzhbeta dances for Doctor Havel,
her grief in the shape of a backside,
a beautiful round and extinct sun
beneath her state uniform.
'What is it Havel?' she sneers,
'did someone die on you?
Look at me now! I'm not dying!'

Doctor Havel is like death.
He takes everything.

But Havel will not take Alzhbeta.
To trip up causality he will
with capricious whimsy he will,
to confound cybernetic prediction he will
reject state nurse Alzhbeta.

The Use of Classical Music

This is the man who, three months before,
had spent two hours mending the holes
in his daughter's pink water-wings
just to see her float across the pool,
legs flourished, chest puffed out to the sky.
Now he has a new skin, green nylon,
reptilian rip-stop. He sits astride
the gun mounting of a pterodactyl-rig,
following sticky traces on his visor.
Loony tune today is the *1812* –

Viet Cong women hear it coming,
strobed above the evening sounds.
Like dreams they run for tree cover
or lie down on their children to die.

Slap-Dash

Up long, winding stairs he has left
his delicate spoor, a smell of meths,
velvet carpet brushed the wrong way.

Evidently he thought he'd have her
reclined and nude, as in books
and films, full length on canvas –

but it seems he is delayed.
Somewhere in a back room,
a night radio lisps quietly

in Old English – a roundness of speech
like falling water
on a plainly painted dish.

Cirque du Grand Bam-Bam

Perhaps on some quiet night
the patter of rain on tarpaulins
and the engineer, driven to distraction,
taking out a curling map
and weighing its corners with books.

His hands and eyes explore
the blank cartography of mangrove levees
and the tense edge of the great imagined ocean
when suddenly he hears
the tremor of palms dancing on drums –
sinking and swelling, vast and faint.

All about him, in muddy delta channels,
drilling barges lie up,
gently tugging at their rotten wharfs.
Nothing seems likely to happen –
yet somehow he is lost,

perhaps in dreams or reverie
or like a genie
in the white smoke of his Camel Lites.

Perhaps on some quiet night
the sound of dancing palms: suggestive, wild,
and barges kissing in the dark,
their orange deck-lights
scorching shadows in the trees
as somewhere someone dies a slow death
by some hitherto unknown disease
and someone shoots himself
and someone else is drowned
under unsuspicious circumstances . . .

At dawn the engineer awakens, chilled,
his own hand printed on his face
in cold relief. The darkness fades,
and palms, if there were palms, stop dancing.

Eyeless in Edgware

Sullivan's heart beat like a miniature asylum bell.
Where were the notes? Where were
the Alka-Seltzer alibis? And more importantly perhaps,
where were the dancing dames?
Sullivan quickened his step.
He did not dare look down at the street,
for he knew, down there, the earth would be spinning
like a greased marble beneath his feet.
He was lost and he knew it.
Suddenly this city, this 'contemporized antique',

had begun to fill him with a sense
of overwhelming nausea.
Sullivan was stuffed, and if Sullivan was stuffed
then so was everybody else.
He stopped and looked from side to side
and saw: the gold shop window, the red satin dress,
the little boy in the blue car,
and the discontinuous yellow stripe down the side of the road.
Coughing fitfully, he stepped into the gutter
and followed it.

Riding the Gun-Box Seat

As on a clear blue morning you wake
and wearing dressing-gown and slippers take
your breakfast on the lawn outside
and there on *The Times* leader page
or there in your correspondence you read,
in unforeseen, dark letters: 'History Made'.

Dismayed, you think of once at Uncle Frank's
when he took you out in his new green Bentley,
through the lanes of County Galway
at hundreds of miles an hour
and you rode the gun-box seat, looking back
at the faces you terrified by going past.

The Solarium Has Exploded

I

Going to bed late, I was
turning the covers, pulling curtains to,
when the emphatic chord of an explosion
entered my head.

This afternoon I saw a dead rat
pushed half through the letterbox
of Gold's solarium –
its tail hung down like a fuse . . .

And now, briefly, the darkened house
has split through like a rotten orange
squirting juice and pips
across Edge Lane, into the night.

II

The fire is furry as a bear.
People fall out of windows. Bats wake
and throw themselves, whistling, into the fire.

The solarium walls collapse and circulate
soft white veils of smoke over
the charred skeleton of rafters.

The night-slippered crowd edges up to the dangerous
                                            shore
where flames break and their own dumb laughter
combusts, wheezily, over their heads.

Fire-engines arrive, fling open their doors
and fill the night sky with grand comic opera.
Three firemen quadrille a pressure hose;

the ladder man is skewered and pushed
like a morsel into the ashes.
They stop at nothing – but nothing stops the fire.

They drown the insect flame,
but the insect flame has grown resistant
to their soda-bright insecticide.

III

Why am I so sad, watching
that ugly solarium burn?
The owner is already rushing home
to write to his insurance company.

I try to make my retreat into sleep
but somehow it seems that more should remain
than the shock of violence at bedtime
and blue lights ebbing past.

I turn up the covers, and wipe some ash
from the bedroom window-sill.
My books are becoming a nuisance,
accumulating on every flat surface.

Some ash has fallen on to an unread passage
which as I brush, is carelessly smudged
to char one or two words
that were once at my fingertips.

In the Hold

What he could not see was the great salon:
a screen by Grinling Gibbons
and all the lovely Lely ladies
gazing down from the panelled walls.
Or after dinner, Ronald Storrs,
telling tales of Europe governed by diplomacy
and Lillah McCarthy, a classical wraith,
reciting Georgian odes.

What he could not see was the dedicated host
charming his band of weekend joysters
from the smoky billiard room
and making haste in settling them
to several swift rounds of charades.

The one, correctly tingling phrase
had always been so difficult to choose.
If that world ever had any substance again
he would know which one he must use.

Biographical Notes

MICHAEL BAYLEY. Born in Bedfordshire in 1952 and has worked in various jobs, including hospital porter and carpet salesman. Spent several years in Paris teaching English. Now lives in Falmouth where he lectures in adult education and runs a poetry workshop. His poems have appeared in *Stand*, the *New Statesman*, *Ambit* and the Gregory Awards anthology. A poem of his was commended in the 1988 National Poetry Competition.

MATTHEW FRANCIS. Born in Hampshire in 1956 and educated at the Universities of Cambridge and Sussex. He has worked as a computer programmer and an author of computer manuals. Three of his stories were published in the Faber collection of new prose writers, *First Fictions: Introduction 10*, and his first novel, *WHOM*, was published in 1989. He has won prizes in several competitions, including the National Poetry Competition.

GRAEME HODGSON. Born in Wallsend in 1961. After leaving home aged sixteen and serving his time as an Engineer Officer in the Merchant Navy he was made redundant and moved to Portsmouth, where he worked in industry. Between 1985 and 1988 he read English at the University of Southampton and followed this up with a teacher training course at the University of London. Currently teaching English at Fareham Tertiary College in Hampshire, he recently married and lives in Southampton.

DAVID MORLEY. Scientist, born in Blackpool in 1964. Descended from a large Romany family; worked in a zoo, and as a barman and bingo-caller. Read Zoology at the University of Bristol (attended Charles Tomlinson's poetry tutorials between science practicals). Won W. E. Frost Fellowship of the Freshwater Biological Association and Queen Mary College, University of London; completed research into the impact of acid rain on Cumbrian lakes and tarns. Founder and director of Poetry Network, an international organization for integrating approaches to science and arts. His poems have appeared in many magazines, most recently *Encounter*, *London Magazine*, *Poetry Now*, *Stand*, *Prospice*, *Rialto*, *Staple* and *The Echo Room*, as well as in five major anthologies and on BBC Radio. His first collection, *Releasing Stone*, was published by The Nanholme Press (amalgamated Giant Steps and Littlewood Press) in July 1989. It won a Tyrone Guthrie Award from Northern Arts in 1988, and a major Eric Gregory Award from the Society of Authors in 1989. *Under the Rainbow*, an exploration of writers and artists in schools, was published by Bloodaxe Books in winter 1989. The poem 'Jackdaw Blues' has been broadcast on the BBC World Service. Along with scientific papers, he has given poetry readings in a wide range of schools and colleges, and is a leader of several workshops in the north of England. Major prize-winner in The Index on Censorship Poetry Competition, 1989, and the Northern Poetry Competition, 1989. Berlin correspondent for several newspapers and magazines during the demolition of the Berlin Wall in November–December 1989.

PAUL MUNDEN. Born in Poole, Dorset, in 1958, he was educated at Canford and the University of York, where he has since run a series of writing workshops. Yorkshire Arts gave him a Writer's Bursary in 1982. His poems have appeared in many magazines, *P.E.N. New Poetry II* and *The Poetry Book Society Anthology 1989*. A pamphlet, *Bonsai*, is published by Aquila. He has won prizes in the Kent Literature Festival and the Yorkshire Open Poetry Competition. In 1987 he received a Gregory Award and now works as a freelance writer. His own imprint, Talking Shop, is to publish poetry cassette/book packs for use in schools. He lives near Castle Howard, Yorkshire, the subject of a sequence of poems, *Henderskelfe*, exhibited with accompanying photographs at Castle Howard in 1989. A cycle of songs has been privately commissioned. He is married, with two young daughters.

ROBERT SAXTON. Born in Nottingham in 1952, he spent his childhood in a village about ten miles north of the city, two miles from Newstead Abbey, Byron's family home. He was educated at Nottingham's Henry Mellish Grammar School and Magdalen College, Oxford, where he held an Exhibition in English and obtained a First class degree. Since then he has worked in publishing. Living in east London, he now holds an executive position in a company producing illustrated books on photography, design, antiques and related subjects. He began writing in 1985. His poems have appeared in various publications, including *Outposts*, *PN Review*, *Poetry Review*, *Oxford Poetry* and the *Spectator*. He won third prize in the *Outposts* Poetry Competition, 1987, for 'River Red with Berries'. In 1988 he won joint first prize in the *TLS*/Cheltenham Festival of Literature Poetry Competition for 'The Promise Clinic'. He also won prizes in 1989 in the Leek Arts Festival Poetry Competition and the Bridport Creative Writing Competition.

JONATHAN TREITEL. Born in London in 1959. He was educated at Stanford University in California, from where he has a Ph.D. in Philosophy of Science and where he studied poetry under Denise Levertov. He has worked as a theoretical quantum physicist. He has travelled extensively in Europe, North America and Asia. His first novel, *The Red Cabbage Café*, is appearing in 1990.

JONATHAN WONHAM.　Born in Glasgow in 1965. Educated at
Gordonstoun School and Imperial College, London. Currently
studying for a Ph.D. in Geology at the University of Liverpool.
His work has previously appeared in *New Statesman*, *Society*,
London Magazine and *Encounter*.